DANGER GUYS:

Hollywood
Halloween

DANGER GUYS:

Hollywood Halloween

by Tony Abbott
illustrated by Suwin Chan

HarperTrophy
A Division of HarperCollinsPublishers

Danger Guys: Hollywood Halloween
Text copyright © 1994 by Robert Abbott
Illustrations copyright © 1994 by Suwin Chan
Suwin Chan's illustrations are inspired by the characters in the cover
painting by Joanne Scribner.

Library of Congress Cataloging-in-Publication Data
Abbott, Tony.
    Danger Guys: Hollywood Halloween / by Tony Abbott ; illustrated by
Suwin Chan.
        p.   cm.
    Summary: When Zeek and Noodle tour the Paragon movie studios
during a thunderstorm, they have all sorts of adventures straight out of
their favorite movies.
    ISBN 0-06-440522-2 (pbk.)
    [1. Motion pictures—Fiction.   2. Adventure and adventurers—Fiction.
3. Halloween—Fiction.]   I. Chan, Suwin, ill.   II. Title.   III. Title:
Hollywood Halloween.
PZ7.A1587Dar   1994   94-8593
[Fic]—dc20   CIP
                                                                    AC

Typography by Stefanie Rosenfeld
2   3   4   5   6   7   8   9   10
❖

For Ernest
for the day when we can
make a movie like this

DANGER GUYS:

Hollywood Halloween

ONE

*B*oom! Ba-boom!*"

"What?"

"That's how it starts," I said. "With lightning flashing and thunder going *Boom! Ba-boom!*"

"Oh. Okay. Go on."

I was in my best friend Zeek's room. He was holding his dad's new video camera. I was telling him my idea for a movie. And, since it was Halloween, it was going to be a scary movie.

"It's dark," I said. "Two kids run into an old house. Their names are Noodle Newton and Zeek Pilinsky."

"The stars!" Zeek smiled as he looked

at me through the camera lens.

"Suddenly, a horrible noise echoes through the house. And Zeek says, '*I'm afraaaid!*' But Noodle stays cool. He says . . ."

"CUT! CUT! CUT!" Zeek said, putting down the camera. "That's not how it goes! I don't say, '*I'm afraaaid.*'"

"Sorry," I said. "I thought one of us should be scared . . . you know . . . a *little*?"

"Well, it can't be me," he said. "Or you, either. We're official Danger Guys. We love this stuff."

It's true. We *are* Danger Guys, and we *do* love this stuff. Action movies, scary movies, adventure movies—we've seen them all. And we've read every book, too.

"Think of something else, Noodle. You're always thinking up something or other."

Yeah, I'm the guy with the ideas. That's why everybody calls me Noodle. And Zeek's the sports whiz, the guy with the muscles.

Together, we are one incredible team.

"Well, okay," I admitted. "How about—"

"Shhh!" Zeek put his finger up to his lips and pointed to his door. The knob turned slowly.

Suddenly—*wham!* The door swung open. I fell behind Zeek's bed. Zeek backed into his desk, tripped, and nearly dropped the camera.

"Got you!" said a familiar voice.

"Dad!" said Zeek. "You scared us!" Then Zeek looked at me and smiled. "Well, not really."

I poked up my head. "We're going to make a Halloween movie with your camera, Mr. P."

"That's why I'm here," he said. "If you plan to make a movie, there's only one place to learn."

Then he held up a handful of tickets. There was a big golden "P" on each one.

Zeek and I looked at each other. We started jumping up and down.

"Paragon Movie Studio!"

Zeek's dad smiled. "That's right. We've got tickets for a tour of the oldest studio in Hollywood. Want to eat first, or—"

Whoosh! We never even heard the rest.

A couple of hours later, Zeek and I, dressed in our Danger Guy jackets, backpacks, and sunglasses, were staring up at the golden letters on the Paragon Studio gate.

"Zeek, look. Just like at the beginning of all those movies. The Paragon gate. Then it fades and the movie starts. Remember *Storm of Terror*? That first scene?"

"Yeah," said Zeek in his deep movie voice. "*'It was a beautiful day. Then something went wrong. Terribly wrong!'* I can't believe it—they made that movie right here!"

"Boys, they made everything here," said Zeek's mom, gazing at Mr. P. "Why, I remember *Strangers in Love* and *Close Friends* and all those other great films. Don't you, dear?"

Zeek and I looked at each other. "Yeah,

 4

I guess they had to make *those* kinds of movies, too."

"And," said Zeek's sister, Emily, "don't forget *Ali Baba*." Then she started to hum the love theme.

Two seconds later, a small bus drove up. We got on with a bunch of other kids and parents.

"Okay, Zeek," I said. "Start rolling. We need some good background shots for our movie."

"Yeah. Too bad it's such a nice day. Maybe we should make a *love* story."

We looked at each other.

"Not!"

"Welcome to Paragon Studio," the driver said as we drove between some huge buildings. "These buildings are called sound stages. Hundreds of movies have been made on these stages. From the first silent films to modern special effects movies, Paragon is the leader!"

"Effects, Noodle," Zeek said. "Like in *Metalhead*, when the cyborg turns into a mailbox right in front of us and the guy goes to open it and—"

"Yes, son, Paragon is known for its special effects," the driver went on. "In fact, many of the monsters and other creatures you see in movies are actually computerized robots. And all of them are run by a central computer here at the Studio. We call it the Big Brain."

Zeek nudged me. "Yeah, like some kind of super Noodle."

I couldn't believe it. "You mean everything is run by this Big Brain?"

"Everything," the tour guide said. "Now here is the castle where they filmed . . ."

Suddenly, the sky turned black above us. I looked up.

Crack! A jagged flash of white light shot down from the clouds. Then—*Boom! Ba-boom!*

"Cool," I said. "Now, that's what I call special effects!"

 6

"Excellent!" said Zeek. "Great opening shot!"

But the driver seemed upset. "These are not effects, boys. That's real lightning. And it's going to rain any second."

He was right. A second later the rain did come down. Real rain. In buckets.

"This way!" the driver shouted. "To the castle!" Everyone jumped off the bus and followed him.

Well, everyone but Zeek and me.

We were too busy trying to get all the rain and lightning on tape. When we stopped looking through the camera, everyone was gone.

"The castle, quick!" I said. "Let's run for it." *Kraaakkk!* A huge bolt of lightning crashed down right in front of us.

Ka-boom! Another blast zapped the street.

"Noodle! This lightning's got a bad attitude!"

Ka-blam!

I whirled around. I saw a door. "Run!" I screamed.

We tore across the street.

We leaped in the air.

We shot through the door as another jagged bolt of lightning blasted our heels.

TWO

Kaaa-*blam!*

We hit the floor, slid into something hard, and stopped dead inside a room. A dark room.

I looked out the door.

There was a big black hole in the street where we had just been. It was smoking like a volcano.

"Holy cow," I said. "Did you see that? That could have been us."

Zeek didn't answer.

His mouth was hanging open.

Just like it does when Mr. Strunk calls on him in class and he's not ready.

I reached over and pushed his mouth

closed.

"But . . . but . . . Noodle!" he mumbled. "This is a movie studio. Nothing *really* dangerous happens here. I mean, does it?"

"Naah," I said. "It's just a storm. When it stops we'll just walk right out, and—"

Bam! A sudden bolt of lightning blasted the street again. *Wham!* A gust of wind slammed the door shut.

"Well, okay, so maybe we don't just walk out."

We looked at the lightning outside the window. It was crashing all over the studio.

"I don't like this, Nood. It's too much like . . ."

"A movie?" I said.

"Yeah, and not a very funny one." Zeek started tripping over things in the dark. "Oww! Where are we, anyway?"

"It's a movie set, I think." I felt the wall near the door, found the light switch, and flicked it. The room suddenly blazed with silver light.

"Whoa! Noodle!" Zeek cried. "I think we just stepped into—the future!"

Zeek was right.

We were standing on the control bridge of the 25th-century galactic star cruiser *Centauri Vulcan*. Well, the movie set of it, anyway. Big cameras, ladders, electrical cables, spotlights, and tools were set up everywhere around the shiny stage.

"Noodle, this is incredible. Look!" Zeek pointed to the end of the set.

There, sparkling in the light, stood the famous transport pods. Each Vulcan movie ended with the crew beaming back into the pods.

"Unbelievable," whispered Zeek. "I want to live here." He pulled out his camera and started taping again.

"It's pretty cool, all right," I said. "But look at this." I was standing at a table near the set. "There are tons of future props here. Space suits, communicators, scanners, fazer guns, flashlights . . ."

"Flashlights? *Ennnh!*" Zeek made a

sound like a game show buzzer. "Wrong! We don't use flashlights in the future. We wear personal ultra-laser-halo-visor things. Nobody uses flashlights anymore! Those are way—"

Ka-blam! More thunder blasted overhead.

The lights on the set flickered and went out. We were in the dark. Totally.

"Oh, man," Zeek groaned. "We should be raccoons, we're in the dark so often. I guess I'll take one of those flashlights . . . "

I felt around in the dark and grabbed two of the flashlights from the table in front of me. I was about to turn one on. Then I heard something.

Tap-tap-tap.

I froze.

"Zeek? Was that you?" I whispered. "Say yes. Please."

"I thought it was you."

Tap. Tap. Tap.

It sounded like metal against metal.

Zeek stumbled over to me. "Just before

the lights went out, I spotted a door across the room."

"Someone's trying to get in," I whispered.

"Yeah, someone. Or some*thing*!"

"I'm going to open it, Zeek. Maybe they'll show us a way out." Zeek grabbed my arm. "No way, Nood." He held me back. "Did you forget the movie we saw last summer?"

I thought for a minute. "We saw *tons* of movies last summer."

"The one with the door. The kid opens it and—" Zeek slipped into his movie voice again. *"They tried to destroy it. But it kept coming back! It's—"*

Blam! A glowing iron fist punched a hole in the door.

"It's—"

Blam! Another fist blasted through.

"It's—"

BLAM! The door blew off its hinges, and a seven-foot monster robot stepped into the room.

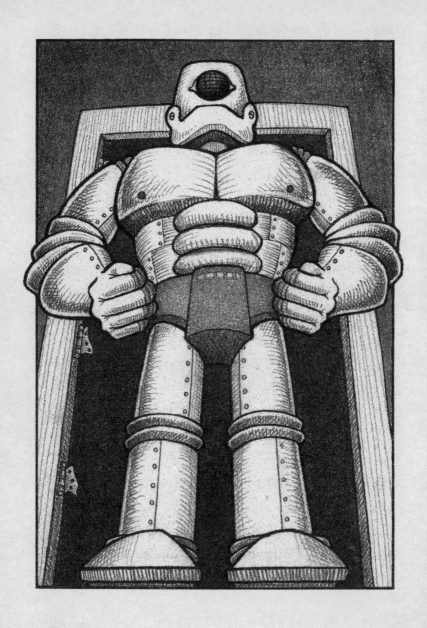

THREE

It's—Metalhead!"

Steel skull for a head. Blinking red eye. It was Metalhead, all right.

And right now that eyeball was scanning the room for human life.

"Hit the deck!" I yelled. We dove across the set and slid under a navigational scanner desk.

"Zeek!" I gasped. "I remember this dude. He's from the future. He's programmed to destroy. That's all he does. I mean, this guy doesn't pump iron. He *is* iron!"

Boom-boom-boom. Metalhead stomped to the center of the room. His eye panned from side to side. Then he started to speak.

"Two humans. Boys. Destroy them."

"Hey," Zeek whispered. "He can't do that. He's an actor!"

"Unh-uh, Zeek. A robot. Remember what the tour guide said. All their monsters are computerized."

Suddenly—*voom!* The desk we were hiding under disappeared. And there was that ugly red eye pulsing down at us.

"Okay, Nood. Be cool. Don't make him mad."

But I had a feeling this dude was *born* mad.

A second later he proved it. He grabbed Zeek, lifted him off the floor, and shook him like a baby rattle.

"Noo-oo-oo-dle!"

"Let go of my pal, Bucket Brain!" I screamed.

I couldn't believe what happened next.

Before I knew it, I jumped up, my leg flew out, and—*wump!*—I gave the big guy a perfect karate kick straight to his knee.

"Yeooow!" My whole body throbbed. But the creep dropped Zeek with a thud.

"Big mistake, human boy." The iron jaw on Metalhead's face grinned an ugly grin.

Suddenly, I realized what I was doing. I was *fighting* with a killing machine from the 21st century! I tried to be nice.

"Sorry, Metalhead. Mr. Metalhead. Sir— I—"

"Don't stand there *talking* to him, Noodle. He's a killer robot! Let's move it!"

"Good call, Zeekie. To the transport deck!"

We sidestepped the big guy and blazed toward the deck at the end of the set. We were making pretty good time.

I was going to give Zeek the old thumbs-up sign. Then we slipped on something. It felt like a skateboard. It wasn't a skateboard.

Whoa! We took off into the air.

"Jetboard!" shouted Zeek. "From *Jump into Time, Part 2*!"

"*Part 3*, you mean."

"Whatever!"

Shooo-ooom! The jet-powered skateboard shot around the control bridge. I dumped the flashlights into Zeek's pack and grabbed his jacket so I wouldn't fall off.

Suddenly we changed direction and blasted off the set and down a dark hall.

"Hey, buddy," I yelled. "I think I see a door at the end of this!"

Wrong. It just looked like a door. It was a wall.

Wham! The jetboard stopped dead. We didn't.

Craaack! We crashed through the wall and tumbled outside into the rain.

I looked back.

There was a cutout in the wall where we had broken through. Two heads, four legs, four arms, and two backpacks. Just like in cartoons.

Stomp! Stomp!

 20

"He's still coming!" Zeek cried.

My brain worked lightning fast. A couple of feet away, there was a puddle of rainwater.

"Excellent," I said. "I've got an idea!"

"Oh, I love when you say that," said Zeek, smiling. Then he frowned. "But where do we hide?"

"We don't. We stick out our feet and wait."

"What?"

Crash! Metalhead blasted through the wall.

Umph! He tripped on our feet.

Splash! His electric head hit the puddle.

Sssssss! Like a burger hitting a hot grill. He twitched a couple times, then stopped moving.

"Well," I said, starting to smile. "I guess that takes care of—"

Blub. Blub. Bubbles came up out of the water.

Zeek stepped closer. "What did he say?"

I looked at my pal.

I gulped.

"He said—'I'll be back!'"

FOUR

Let's get out of here," said Zeek.

He didn't have to say that twice.

We jumped the puddle and bolted down a narrow muddy path. The lightning had almost stopped, but it was still raining pretty hard.

We ducked under a leafy tree.

"Okay," said Zeek. "Time out. What was all that about anyway? I mean, Shovel Face wasn't really trying to kill us. Was he?"

I shook my head. "I don't know."

"Or maybe it's just some kind of Halloween show the studio is putting on. You know, to scare us?"

Thunder rumbled over our heads.

"Maybe," I said. But something told me, maybe not. "But I think we'd better get to the castle and tell everybody what happened."

Zeek nodded. "Where are we, anyway?"

I did a quick look around. Big green ferns and leafy plants grew up on each side of the path. Tall skinny trees with lots of vines towered above us into the mist. The rain pattered on the leaves.

"A jungle," I said.

I pushed through some bushes. "I think there's a building up there. The castle is probably just around the corner." I smiled and poked up my thumb. Zeek did the same.

We made our way through the jungle. Zeek swung his camera all around at the wild plants. "Maybe we could make a jungle movie. *Noodle, the Ape Boy* or something like that."

"Ha, ha," I said. "Let's just keep going."

But when we got to the building, there

wasn't any. Building, I mean. It was just a wall, painted to look like a building.

"Whoa!" said Zeek.

"I agree," I said. Then I swallowed hard and started back into the jungle. "This isn't really happening."

"Sorry, Nood," said Zeek, tapping his video camera. "It's happening. I've got it all on tape."

Lightning flashed in the distance. The rain dripped down through the leaves as we walked.

"I wish I knew why Metalhead attacked us," I said. "I don't really think it was part of the Paragon Studio experience."

"But what could make him go so crazy?" Zeek said. "The lousy weather?" He smiled.

"Yeah, right," I said. Then I looked up at the sky. Something was starting to click in my head.

We pushed through a thick wall of leaves and into a clearing. At the center was a huge black boulder.

"All right," I said, running over to it. "We should be able to see the castle from here."

We clambered up the rock, stood on top, and looked around.

"Cool view!" Zeek took out the video camera again and started panning around.

The view was cool, all right.

We could see the whole studio from there. To our left was the western town where they filmed *Trigger Happy*. Next to it was the lake from *Swamp Creep* and the streets of Metro City where they made *Catman* and *Catman Returns*.

Not too far away was an old broken-down house. I didn't like the look of that house. It made my skin crawl.

But just behind it was the castle.

"Bingo," I said. "In three minutes we're there."

"Yeah, just wait until they hear what happened to us."

We started down from the boulder.

"You know, Zeek," I said. "I've been

thinking about what happened with Metal-head. I haven't figured it all out yet, but—"

Suddenly, the boulder shifted a little.

"Whoa, Zeek! Did you feel anything?"

Zeek looked at me. "The Paragon Earthquake ride? I thought that opens next summer."

I looked down at the rock under our feet. The surface started to *wrinkle*. Then it stretched out. Then it—breathed!

"No . . ." I mumbled. "I don't think it's an earthquake."

All of a sudden, a huge black scaly head the size of a bus swung around at us and roared!

"Grrraaaooowww!"

"Gorgatron!" yelled Zeek.

"What?" I shouted. "You know this guy?"

"Gorgatron! The prehistoric dino-lizard they made for *Gorgatron Park*! It's hungry. And we're on its back!"

Zeek was right. We were on its back. And it did look hungry.

Suddenly, Gorgatron bent over to see what was for lunch. It looked right in Zeek's camera.

"Extreme close-up!" Zeek screamed.

Then the dinosaur made a strange noise.

"Kerr-kerrr-kerrr—"

"No!" yelled Zeek. "Not that! It's going to—to—"

"—Phlooooo!"

It sneezed all over us.

"Grossssss!" we both screamed, as the force blew us down the dino's back in a river of goop.

Gorgatron rose up on its hind legs. We tumbled to the ground.

"Oh, man," Zeek moaned. "Of all the futuristic attack weapons, we had to choose flashlights!"

I looked over at him. "Yeah, right," I yelled. "Like we're really going to fight him!"

"Grrraaaooooooowww!"

Gorgatron stretched up about fifty feet

in the air. He began to chase us.

Wump-wump-wump! The ground thundered beneath the huge weight.

Zeek and I raced back into the jungle. I could hear leaves and trees crashing right behind us. The beast was hot on our tails.

"Hurry!" I shouted. "I read that dinos could run really fast!"

Wump-wump-wump!

"Yeah?" yelled Zeek. "And did you get to the part that tells how to escape from one?"

We dashed back into the clearing again.

"Over there!" Zeek pointed to the old broken-down house. "Let's move it—fast!"

"No way," I yelled. "I mean that house is all falling down and dark inside and really creepy and I think maybe it's been used for every haunted house movie since time began and—"

"Grrrraaaaaoooooooowwwww!"

"But hey, with a little paint—"

FIVE

We flashed across the clearing, flew up the steps, and dived through the front door of the old house.

The door wasn't open, but like I said—the place was old.

We collapsed in the living room of the number-one haunted house in America.

"I have a bad feeling about this," I said.

Zeek nodded. "But at least we don't have ugly monster killer dino-bots chasing us."

He had a point. I went over to the window. Gorgatron was thumping back into the jungle. "Even he's afraid of this place," I said.

In the dim light I could see that the walls were dark and stained. There were cobwebs all over everything. There were wobbly-looking stairs going up to the next floor. And the room had a really bad smell.

"Hey," said Zeek, looking around from behind his video camera. "They made *Nutzoid* here."

I turned to Zeek. "Of course they made *Nutzoid* here! And *Bobby Hammerhands*. And *Cold Sweat*. And *Oozeface*. And—"

"Arrrgh."

"What?" I said.

"I didn't say anything," said Zeek.

"Yes, you did. You said 'Arrrgh.'"

Zeek looked at me. "That wasn't me. I wouldn't say that, honest. Why would I say that?"

"Arrrgh."

I looked at him closely, trying to see his mouth move. "You're trying to scare me, aren't you, Zeek. We're in a haunted house and you're trying to scare me. Pretty soon you'll be saying things like—"

"Mum . . . mum . . . mum . . ." Zeek stuttered.

"No, not 'mum-mum-mum'," I said. "Scary things. Things like 'IIIEEE!' or—"

"Mum . . . mum . . . mum . . ." he said again. He obviously wasn't listening to me. And he wasn't looking at me either. He was looking over my shoulder. His eyes were going kind of buggy.

"Arrrgh!"

"What *is* that noise?" I said. I finally looked around. A man was thumping down the stairs. An old man. Very old. He was very dusty. And he was wrapped from head to foot in—well—toilet paper!

"ARRRGH!" he groaned.

"Oh, a mummy," I said. "Zeek, it's a—"

"IIIEEE!"

Wham! The door banged and Zeek disappeared down a hall. I heard him slam a door and start piling up stuff on the other side of it.

I looked down the hall. I looked at

the guy coming down the stairs. I wasn't getting it.

"Wait a minute," I said to the old guy. "You're dressed up, right? I mean, it's Halloween and you're dressed up. Right? RIGHT?"

"Arrrgh!" was all he said. Then he slowly stretched out one of his creepy arms. He thumped across the room toward me. He was leaving little clouds of dust with every step.

I tried to be nice, but when he stretched out his other creepy arm toward me, I had to be rude.

Wham! I blasted from the room into the hall.

"Arrrgh!" said the mummy. And he started down the hall after me.

I got to the room where Zeek was hiding. I banged on the door. "Zeek! It's me! Let me in!"

"How do I know it's you?" Zeek yelled through the door. "How do I know you're not a mummy who just sounds like you!"

"Because mummies can only say 'Arrrgh!' Now open up or I'll—"

"Arrrgh!"

The mummy was getting closer. I was trapped against the door. Those ugly arms were stretched out toward me.

"Zeeeeeekie!" I screamed. "The dead guy!"

Suddenly, the door flew open, and I tumbled into the room with Zeek. He slammed the door behind me and pushed chairs and tables and other stuff back in front of it.

I was safe.

"Whew!" I gasped. "That was close."

"Too close," said Zeek. Then he looked at my jacket. "So he got you, huh?"

"Who?"

"Him. Out there. The mummy."

"No way!" I said. "He didn't get me. I wouldn't let that old bag of bones get me. No way."

"Oh yeah?" Zeek blew on my shoulder and a puff of white mummy dust floated up.

SIX

I gulped. And pushed another chair in front of the door. Then I turned around and saw Zeek video taping me.

"Come on, pal," I said. "No more fooling around. We've got to get out of here."

Zeek nodded and stuffed the video camera in his backpack. "Good call, Noodle. What's the plan?"

I looked around. "First, I need a minute to figure out what's going on. Then I'll think up a plan."

I sat down on an old couch. Dust flew up. "I mean, it's like we're in some really bad Halloween movie, you know? And everybody is trying to kill us. But why?"

Zeek just shook his head. "Because they know we're Danger Guys and we love this kind of stuff?"

I smiled. "That would be cool. But, I don't think so." I looked at the white spot on my shoulder. "Nope, this is a little too real."

The sky rumbled outside. The storm was going to be a long one. Then, I thought of something. "Hmmm," I said. "No way. It couldn't be. It's just too—nutty."

Zeek came over and slumped down next to me. Dust flew up again. "All right, Noodle. You got me. Let's hear it."

"Well," I said. "It's crazy, but the tour guide said that all the special effects and creatures were run by a big central computer, right?"

"Yeah. The Big Brain. So?"

"So," I said, "what if that lightning storm we had zapped the Brain? And it starts making these creatures go crazy. They're all robots, remember? And the

Brain controls them."

Zeek was quiet for a second. "You mean like a short circuit in the computer? There sure was a lot of lightning."

"Exactly. Electrical storms do pretty strange things. Remember the storm in *Evil Experiment*? The wacko doctor puts the dead guy out in the lightning and— zap—he's alive! And he's dangerous, too, just like—"

Suddenly Zeek stood up. "But that means—oh no! My parents! My sister! What if some crazy robot monster attacks the castle? We're Danger Guys. But them, they're just regular people!"

I looked at Zeek. He was scared.

So was I.

Then I smelled it. I grabbed Zeek's arm.

He sniffed too. "Cooking. Someone is cooking in this house. Maybe they can help us!"

There was a door on the far side of the room. My stomach told me that was the way. I opened the door slowly. We looked into—a kitchen.

It was different from the other rooms in the house. It was cleaner. Brighter. It almost looked like a normal room.

But the most amazing part was that there was a woman in the room. She looked normal, too. Like a regular person. Like a regular mom.

"I think we lucked out, pal," I whispered to Zeek. "She must work here. She can help us!"

We stepped into the kitchen. Zeek gave me a quick thumbs-up and nodded.

"Excuse me, ma'am," I said. "We need help. Really strange things have been happening to us and my friend's parents are in danger and—"

The woman looked over and smiled at us.

"Come in, boys," she said. "I'll call the police right away. But first, sit down and have something to eat. Waffles okay?"

I looked at Zeek. "I must have died and gone to heaven. She said waffles!"

I smiled big.

Waffles are my absolute favorite food.

Zeek could probably see the hunger in my eyes. "Two bites," he said. "Then the police."

"Of course," the woman said. She seemed nice.

Zeek and I sat down at the table.

The woman turned on a radio and hummed to the music. She stepped over to the counter, picked up two plates, and set them on the table.

Dun-dun-dunnn! The music on the radio suddenly changed. It got creepy.

And so did the lady's face. Her mouth twisted all up. Then her eyes blinked and rolled backward.

"Noodle! She's one of *them*! RUN!"

We jumped for the door.

Wham! Too late. "Dad" was there.

"Hunnneee!" he groaned as he stood in the doorway. "I'mmm home!"

Oh, sure. Just your ordinary, everyday Dad.

Only this one had a flat head, a huge scar, and little silver electrodes sticking out of his neck.

"Get them, Frank!" the lady snapped.

"We're out of here!" I shouted.

Before dear old Dad could stretch out his huge arms for us, we were blurring through the kitchen and up the stairs.

"Bathroom!" Zeek yelled.

"We don't have time," I shouted.

"No—the bathroom window! It's open!"

Stomp. Stomp. Stomp. Flathead Dad was storming up the stairs.

We shot into the bathroom. But when we tried to climb out the window, it wasn't. A window, I mean. It was just painted on the wall.

"Yikes!" yelled Zeek. "Up the stairs!"

We flew up three more flights of old-creaking-loose-falling-down stairs.

"Oh, man, Zeek," I huffed. "This is not happening!"

"You can say that all you want, Nood. But it keeps on happening!"

When we got to the top floor, I ran in the first room I could find. I pulled Zeek in behind me, and locked the door.

Big mistake.

"Grrrrrr!"

"Noodle?" Zeek said. "That's your stomach, right? You saw the waffles, you didn't eat them, and now your stomach is growling, right?"

"Um . . . sorry, Zeek."

"Grrrrrr-rrrrrrr!"

We looked over to the bed. Someone was waking up. He didn't look too happy. He also didn't look too human. He was all hairy, like a—

"Werewolf!"

The werewolf bolted up, sprang in front of Zeek, and threw him toward the window. *Crash!*

"Noooooooooodle!"

I froze in shock as I saw Zeek break through the window and go tumbling out.

All the way to the ground.

Four floors below.

45

SEVEN

You creep!" I screamed. "You killed my best friend!"

I jumped on the bed, bounced up and kicked the hairy jerk with both feet.

The wolfman slumped over. But the force of the kick knocked me off the bed. I hit a chair, flipped over, and flew out the window, too.

Whoa! I grabbed the windowsill and hung on. But my grip was no good.

I couldn't hold on.

My fingers slipped off the edge.

"Ahhhhh!" I fell straight down.

A second later, something grabbed me.

"Don't worry, Noodle. I've got you!"

It was Zeek!

I looked down. There was nothing but air below us. "You've got me?" I said. "But who's got you?"

Vooom!

We fell like rocks.

Boing!

We bounced back up again.

"It's a stunt trampoline, Nood! So when the heroes fall out of windows, they don't get hurt!"

Boing!

"I can't believe it!" I cried. "Does this mean that Danger Guys are indestructible?"

"Well, so far, anyway!" Zeek said, giving me a smile. Then he pointed down. "A couple more jumps, and we're out. Look!"

About twenty feet away was a regular backyard. And across the yard was the castle.

"Let's hop!" I shouted.

We bounced a couple more times, somersaulted, and landed in the backyard.

"Um . . . Noodle?" said Zeek, dusting himself off. "This isn't your ordinary backyard."

I looked around. It *was* pretty gloomy for a backyard. All twisted trees and statues of angels.

"Oh, great," I said. "A graveyard. And just when I thought we were—"

"Boneheads!" Zeek screamed.

"Well," I huffed. "I wouldn't say that!"

"Not us. Them!" Zeek pointed behind me. There, pouring up from one of the graves, like clowns from a taxi, were skeletons!

Dozens of skeletons! And each one carried a long jagged sword.

We jumped behind a skinny tree.

"Uh-oh," Zeek whispered. "These guys are no good. Remember *Boneheads vs. Elm City*? They got mad and wanted people to dress like them."

"Yeah, well, I don't look good in just bones," I said, trying to make myself skinnier than the tree.

Suddenly, the skeletons turned. They spotted us. They got into line and began marching toward us. They raised their swords.

"Zeekie," I whispered. "I don't think this looks too—"

Kraaack! A bolt of lightning flashed suddenly through the sky.

Instantly, the skeletons stopped. The whole army of them turned completely around on their bony heels. They began to march away.

"But . . ." I started to say.

Then Zeek grabbed my arm. He pointed to where the skeleton army was going.

I watched them march across the yard.

"*The castle!* Noodle! My folks are in there!"

EIGHT

Step on it!" Zeek shouted as we ran. "Pretend you're in *The Black Knight!*"

I watched as the last of the Boneheads trooped into the castle. The huge drawbridge was closing up in front of us.

We had only one chance to make it. Speed was the thing. And Zeek's folks were in danger.

So I took a running start, stretched out my arms, and jumped. Up.

It worked. We grabbed the top of the drawbridge, and it pulled us all the way up to the top of the castle wall.

A second later, I was standing next to

Zeek on a walkway overlooking the castle courtyard.

Clack! Clack!

Below us, the Boneheads were marching in.

"Noodle, they're searching for the tour group. We've got to get down there, and fast!"

I nodded and pointed to an opening in the wall. "This way looks good." We scrambled over to the doorway and ran down some steps.

Big mistake.

Because when we leaped down to the floor, it wasn't there. The floor, I mean.

It fell away while we were in midair. Just like every trap door in every castle movie I've ever seen.

"No!" I yelled.

Umph! *Umph*! We dropped about twenty feet and crumpled in a pile.

"Noodle?" Zeek groaned. "I think you found us a dungeon!"

It sure looked like a dungeon. Small

room. No doors or windows. Chains on the walls. Yeah, it was a dungeon all right.

"This looks kind of like the torture chamber in *Zorando's Revenge*," said Zeek.

"No," I said. "It's more like the one in *Zorando's End*. But I hope it's not that one because that's the one where the walls—"

Clank-clank-clank.

A loud noise filled the room. It sounded like chains and rocks grinding together.

I looked at Zeek. Then I looked behind Zeek. "Um . . . do you notice anything strange?"

"You mean, like the walls are getting closer?"

"Yeah, and do you know what that means?"

"*Zorando's End*?"

"Right. It means we're in—in— "

"The Squishing Room!"

"HELLLLLLLLLLLLP!"

Our yells echoed through the castle.

No one answered.

In a flash we were up against the walls, pushing hard. Zeek's muscles bulged. I helped, too.

No good. We just slid back across the floor. The walls kept coming.

Slowly, but surely, we'd be crushed to death.

"This is it," said Zeek. "We're doomed."

I had to admit it didn't look good for us. The hole in the ceiling was way too far away. No one heard our cries for help.

"And the worst part is," Zeek said, "we won't be able to save my parents or the other people on the tour. The Boneheads are probably closing in on them right now."

The walls slid closer. We slumped to the floor.

Zeek looked over at me. "Well, buddy, if this is the end, at least we'll be together."

"Yeah," I said, looking at the walls closing in. "We'll be so together, they won't be able to tell us apart!"

Zeek laughed. He stuck his thumb up in

the air, for maybe the last time. I did the same.

Then he took out the video camera and pointed it at me. "Any last words?"

I jumped up. "That's it!"

"What's it?"

"If we were in a real movie, what would we do to save ourselves? I mean, we're Danger Guys! We're the heroes here!"

Zeek sat up. "Well, we'd probably have some cool props to help us out? Like maybe a ladder."

"That would be too easy. Let's check our backpacks. We've got to have something!"

Zeek opened his. "Blank tapes. Extra battery. Sunglasses. Those two flashlights from the *Vulcan*. Not much. What's in yours?"

"I don't even know. My dad packed it this morning." I turned it upside down and one thing dropped out on the floor.

Clunk!

"A lunch box? Oh yeah, Noodle. What every hero needs."

"Hey, not just any lunch box. My official Indiana Jones lunch box. We can eat while we think."

I opened the box and took out a peanut-butter-and-jelly sandwich made on waffles. That's a specialty my mom makes me because she knows about me and waffles.

I gave half of it to Zeek as the walls slid closer.

"Last meal?" he asked me.

I tried to smile.

Then, I had a brilliant idea. The most brilliant idea ever. I mean, the reason they call me Noodle is because of ideas like these. This idea—

"Hurry, Nood. It's getting a little tight in here!"

Okay. I opened the lunch box face down on the floor between the crushing walls. It was right underneath the hole that we had fallen through.

"Perfect," I said. "Now we stand on it, one foot on the front, one on the back. And we wait." I smiled big. "Simple!"

"Simple death, you mean!"

"Hey, pal," I said. "It's our only hope. Now hand me a flashlight. If this goes the way I want it to, we'll need something to bonk some skullheads."

"And if it doesn't go the way you want it to?"

I shrugged. "Then we'll be human mush in—ten seconds."

"Tough choice. Not!" Zeek jumped up with me on the lunch box.

Clank-clank-clank. The walls came closer.

Six feet. Five feet. Four feet. Three feet.

"Noodle, I just want to say that you're my best friend in the whole world and we've had the greatest times and if we did it all over again I wouldn't change a—a—aaaeeeooowww!"

CRRRRRUUUUUUUNCH!

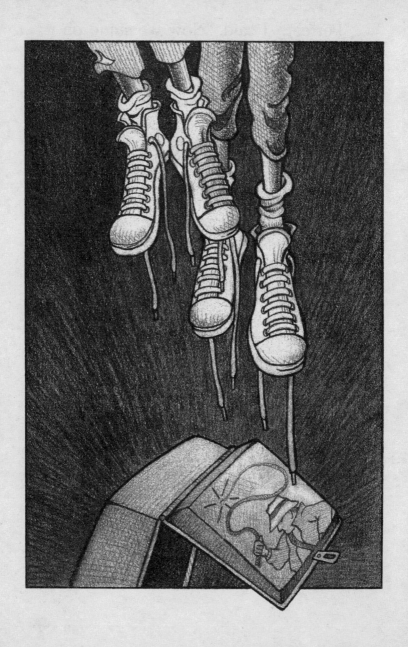

NINE

The walls hit the lunch box. They made a horrible grinding sound. They kept squeezing—squeezing—squeezing—

SNAP!

My lunch box snapped closed with such force we shot like rockets right through that hole in the ceiling just as the walls came crashing together!

Instantly we found ourselves in a hall in the castle surrounded by fifty Boneheads.

Their empty jaws were grinning at us. Their swords waved in the air in front of our noses.

"Wipe those smiles off your skulls, you creeps! You're up against Danger Guys now!"

I held up my flashlight and shook it in their faces.

Suddenly—*fwing!* An icy shaft of blue light shot out of the open end.

The Boneheads stepped back.

"Whoa, Zeekie! It's not a flashlight!"

Zeek hit a switch on his, and the light flung out instantly. "Laser swords! Noodle! Just like they used in *Space Wars!*"

The blades hummed as we moved them back and forth through the air. Sparks flew off them.

Zeek smiled.

I smiled too. We were thinking the same thing.

"Swordfight!"

Clang! Clink! Chong!

It was incredible.

"The Power is with us!" we shouted, as we drove the skeletons back into the main hall.

Instantly we saw Zeek's parents, his little sister, and all the others huddling against the wall near some long curtains.

"Hooray!" they cheered when they saw us.

"Good audience," Zeek yelled.

Our swords whizzed through the air like helicopter blades. We were like Rick Starmover and Hal Sono in *Space Wars: The Return*.

I laughed out loud, thrust my sword straight out, and spun around on my sneaker.

Clack-plink-snap-crunch! Four skeletons bit the dust! I twirled again. Two more crashed to the floor.

Another Bonehead clattered over and started waving his sword at us.

"Yeah," snorted Zeek. "As if—!"

Clang! Zeek slammed him on the head. Sparks went up. Bony went down.

"Ha-ha!" I yelled. "There's no stopping the forces of justice and goodness and right and—"

"Emily!" Mr. Pilinsky screamed.

I looked up to see one of the

Boneheads chasing Zeek's sister up the stairs to the balcony.

"I'll save her!" I shouted.

I leaped onto a stuffed chair, bounced high, pulled myself up to the balcony, and jumped down between Emily and the Bonehead. I waved my sword and grinned at him.

But the Bonehead grinned, too. He chopped down with his jagged blade. I swung my laser sword up. *Clank!* Sparks showered all around. I leaped up to the balcony railing and walloped the bone guy on the head.

He didn't like that. He climbed up to the railing, too. I thrust my sword straight at him. Too bad for him he didn't have rubber-soled extra-grip sneakers. He slipped backward, I tapped him once more with my sword, and he toppled over the side. *Crash!* He shattered on the floor.

"My hero!" Emily cried. She ran to safety, clapping the whole way. Boy, that felt good.

But when I turned to run down the stairs, three more Boneheads were grinning at me.

My laser sword started to sputter. Then it died out.

"Uh-oh!" I gasped.

The Boneheads held out their swords and lunged at me but—incredibly—they crumpled to the floor at my feet.

"Ha! Scared you, didn't I?" I smirked.

Then I saw the real reason.

Emily. She was smiling and holding out a curtain rope. "I tripped them," she said. "Is that okay?"

"Unbelievably okay! I—"

"Noooooooodle!" cried Zeek. His laser was fizzling out too. I jumped down to help him.

But when the Boneheads saw that we had no weapons, they backed us up against the wall.

They waved their long swords in our faces. They grinned their ugly grins at us.

And they came in for the kill.

65

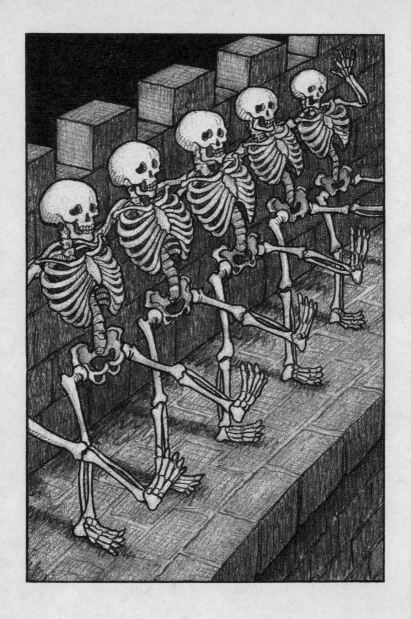

TEN

Zeek looked over at me. "Any last words?"

"I've got an idea!"

"I like those words."

I grabbed Zeek's backpack, pulled out the video camera, pointed it at the bone guys, and turned it on. "Lights! Camera! Action!" I yelled.

What happened next was a truly amazing video experience.

The Boneheads stopped just inches from us. They lifted their heads all at once. Then they linked their bony arms together, kicked their feet from side to side, and started to dance!

"Score one for the Noodster!" Zeek cried. "A chorus line! Pal, you're brilliant. Of course they're going to act for the camera—they're movie stars!"

Yeah, sometimes I amaze even myself.

I started talking like a director. "Okay, fellas, out of the hall, outside, and up to the wall."

The Bonehead chorus was creaky, but they were professionals. They danced just where we told them to go.

A couple of seconds later we were up on the outside walkway around the castle.

"Hey, Zeek, this directing thing is cool!" I said, waving the skeletons back. "A little farther left, gentlemen! A little more. A little more—!"

Splash! The whole army of Boneheads went crashing over the wall and into the moat below.

"Hooray!" came a cheer from the courtyard.

"All right, Noodle! We did it. We saved

 68

everybody. Some incredible day, wasn't it?"

I just looked at Zeek and shook my head.

"Why are you shaking your head? I don't like that. We're done here, Noodle. Aren't we?"

"Nice try," I said. "The Big Brain, remember?"

Zeek made a face, but he knew I was right.

When we got to the main hall, I talked to the tour guide. He told me what I needed to know.

"The Big Brain is right in this castle, son. But you can't go in alone. It's a powerful computer, and after a storm like this, it could do anything."

"Thanks," I said. "But, we've got to shut it down before someone really gets hurt."

I turned to Zeek's mom and dad. "We'll meet you all at the Paragon gate. My pal and I have a job to finish." I was getting really excited.

"We'll send help!" Mrs. P. called over

her shoulder. Everybody ran for the entrance.

Zeek tapped me on the shoulder. "But help won't get here in time, will it, Nood?"

I shook my head.

"And we could face even worse dangers in there, right?"

"Yeah," I said. "We could."

"So it's a journey into the unknown, isn't it?"

"Absolutely."

We just looked at each other for a long time.

We started to smile.

Those old thumbs jabbed up.

"Let's do it!"

ELEVEN

Within seconds, we were deep in the castle. We crept along quickly and silently. Torches high on the walls flickered and shadowed the way.

"Noodle, I've got a bad feeling about this."

We rounded a corner and found ourselves facing an enormous set of iron doors.

"I've got a feeling, too," I said. "We're here."

Zeek looked at me. He didn't smile. But he did shove his thumb up. I nodded and did the same.

"Together, then. One. Two. Three!"

The huge doors swung open without a sound. Inside was a long room. The ceiling was fifty feet high. The floor was made of shiny marble.

Along each of the side walls were long red curtains. The place looked like a throne room.

Except that at the far end, taking up a whole wall, was a giant computer. It was the size of thirty refrigerators. Sparks were shooting off it like fireworks and fizzling on the floor.

The whole thing was glowing.

"The Big Brain!" I said. "Boy, that lightning must have zapped it pretty good."

"I can see the switch," Zeek whispered. "Let's shut this baby off and blow it up. Simple."

"Too simple," I muttered, stepping toward the computer. I was right.

Boom! Ba-boom! A bolt of lightning suddenly blasted down in front of us. Then another.

The whole room started to quake.

 74

Thunder exploded from every corner.

"Noodle! It's the end of the world!"

WHOOM! One enormous wall burst into flames like a tidal wave. Then another and another exploded into fire until we were completely surrounded.

There was no escape. Thunder rumbled and lightning crackled all around us. The air filled with black smoke.

"Zeeekie!" I shouted. "Where are you?"

"Nooodle!" he yelled. *"I'm afraaaid!"*

Then—in a blinding flash—it came to me.

It was another one of those golden moments. I laughed out loud at my idea.

The walls of fire were closing in on us, the lightning was exploding, the thunder crashed and boomed.

I jumped up and shouted.

"CUT! CUT! CUT!"

Instantly, the fire storm vanished. The thunder silenced. The lightning stopped.

Everything went quiet. The room was just like it was before.

Zeek looked up. "Noodle? What—?"

"Effects, Zeek," I said. "Special effects. The computer thought it was the climax to a horror movie. All we had to do was stop the movie."

Zeek jumped up and down. "Noodle! You're brilliant. You saved us!"

"Unh-uh, pal," I said, smiling. "You did."

"Me?"

"Yeah, remember this morning when I was telling you my story? Remember what I made you say?"

"Oh yeah!" said Zeek. "You told me to say, '*I'm afraaaid.*'"

"Right," I said. "Then you said, 'CUT!' That was the magic word. All I did was remember it."

"Hey, we did it together! We are one incredible team!" Zeek punched his thumb in the air and laughed. So did I.

Fssssss! The Big Brain sizzled. Sparks flew off in different directions.

I looked at Zeek. "All we have to do

 76

now is shut off that overheated pile of junk and we're home free."

"Right," said Zeek. But he didn't move.

The lights on the Big Brain flickered. It seemed like it was watching us.

"Right," I said. "Let's do it." I didn't move either.

Finally Zeek said, "Hey, what could happen?"

I smiled. Yeah, what could happen?

We walked slowly over to the computer. The Big Brain was hot. It was fizzling and growling to itself, as if it were mad.

"There's the switch," I said, pointing to a small red button.

We reached forward. *Click*. We shut it off together.

The sparks died.

The fizzling stopped.

The Big Brain went to sleep.

Suddenly—*swoosh!* The curtains along the walls opened. And golden afternoon sunlight streamed across the floor.

"Whoa!" said Zeek. "As if it never really happened."

"Maybe it didn't," I said with a smile. "After all—this *is* Hollywood!"

Everyone cheered and clapped when we got to the front gate. Zeek's mom and dad and sister gave us both big hugs.

Then the owner of the studio came over to us. He was glad we were all safe. He thanked us for saving everyone. "We'll be doing a complete overhaul of our computer system," he told us.

"Yeah." Zeek smiled. "It has a severe attitude problem!"

Then the owner did an incredible thing. He said that Paragon Studio would like to make a movie with the tape from our camera!

"You boys wouldn't mind being movie stars, would you?"

I didn't have to think twice. Neither did Zeek.

We slid our sunglasses on and smiled big.

"Where's our limo?" I said.

That's when we heard it.

Two little kids from the tour were playing by the front gate while they were waiting to go home.

"Okay," one kid said. "This time, I play Noodle and you play Zeek!"

"Coool!" the other kid said. Then he climbed the famous Paragon gate and did our thumbs-up sign.

"Danger!" he screamed.

I looked at Zeek. He looked at me.

"Noodle?" he said. "Who needs movies? We're living the real thing!"

I smiled at him.

Yeah.

Danger Guys.

The legend continues.

Don't miss the next dangerous adventure:

DANGER GUYS

Hit the Beach

🌴 Noodle and Zeek are chillin' at the beach with their surfer dude pal, Boomer.

🌴 One crazy wave lands their surfboard on a deserted island where they discover the dusty bones of sea captain John May.

🌴 A cutthroat gang of thieves is planning to steal the fortune in gold that sank with Captain May's ship.

🌴 With a little help from a sea monster with a bad attitude, it's the Danger Guys to the rescue!